Naughty Ladies

of the

Pearly Gates

Deserving Angels of Montana

Karen Carpenter

Tobacco River Ranch
P.O. Box 1570
Eureka, MT 59917

Credits:

Book Design and Composition: Barbara A. Swanson, Pica^2 Graphics,
    Colorado Springs, CO
Cover Illustration and Art: Karen Carpenter
Edit and Project Management: Sharon Green, Panache Editorial, Inc.,
    Colorado Springs, CO
Printed by FC Printing, West Valley City, UT

First Edition
First Printing, 2006

ISBN: 0-9773339-0-6

Tobacco River Ranch
P.O. Box 1570
Eureka, MT 59917

Printed in the United States of America, 2006

Karen Carpenter
11/26/05

Naughty Ladies
of the
Pearly Gates

Table of Contents

Dedication

To the ladies of all sizes and races and temperaments, who created an atmosphere of warmth and companionship in an otherwise rough-and-tumble world. We salute you, Belle and all the Ladies of the Pearly Gates, for your bravery and compassion.

Foreword

I am very happy to tell you how this book came to be. Karen Carpenter, a well-known artist in the Kallispel–Eureka, Montana area, and I have worked together for some years on various projects. She has a tremendous talent. From time to time I find that she is able to predict the kind of things I like and she brings me pieces that must have been made just for me. Over the years I have accumulated a fair number of Karen Carpenter pieces, which I am delighted to have.

I have also commissioned Karen do to a variety of pieces, mostly figures but on occasion some landscapes of the area. The first piece I had her do was her interpretation of the female warrior described in Conrad's *Heart of Darkness*. More recently, I had her do a similar project that involved her visualization of a fictional account of a young lady who was taken captive in the 1800s and forced to serve in a harem for a very powerful desert sheik.

Early this year, Karen brought me a charcoal drawing of four charming ladies draped all over each other. She referred to them as her Hurdy-Gurdy gals. The composition, facial expressions, and depiction of the ladies, who had moved beyond their physical prime and for whom gravity had taken its toll, were absolutely wonderful. She had captured their essence and their spirit like I had never seen before. I bought the piece and suggested to Karen that she do three more charcoals of similar ladies. I thought they would make excellent subject matter for another pictorial project I had in mind.

With each charcoal Karen sent to me she included a paragraph describing the lady. It didn't take long to realize that this fine artist, whose ability to draw the human form was already apparent, also could channel her amazing talent into language. She could write, and she was witty and imaginative as well as sensitive to her subject matter. I wrote to Karen and made an appointment to visit her to discuss yet another project that seemed far more worthy of her obvious talent.

Karen, Wayne, and I met and talked about different ideas for a book about these ladies. It would be a book for which Karen would be both author and artist. We came to the conclusion that readers would be more inclined to be more interested in a book about ladies with an unusual past than about these ladies after they were turned out to pasture. The more art Karen sent me, the more copy I wanted to read. So Karen started writing more about our "naughty" ladies. Very soon I was looking forward to reading the text as much as to looking at the pictures.

I sent the material to Sharon Green, an excellent editor, who I somehow felt could deal with the somewhat risqué nature of Karen's copy. Karen and Sharon may be two of the ladies in the book, but I'll never tell. The combination has been wonderful to behold. Almost better than that has been watching Wayne, Karen's partner and emotional support, get involved and eventually gain enough self-confidence to tell Karen how he really feels about her.

When you finish reading this volume, you'll be crying for the next one—and it won't be far behind. So, hang onto your hats and settle down to a fun read while Belle tells you a story and gives you some sage advice. If you are like me, we are all sorely in need of good advice, no matter what the source.

Gary Paul Cox

Preface

I can remember a day many years ago when I met lady who smiled at me and said, "I can make anything into a piece of art." By golly, after being with that lady for many years, I've seen Karen Carpenter turn many a thing into a piece of fine art.

This book is an example of her exceptional talents. These lovely ladies are something that Karen has carried in her mental files for many years.

After decades of creating pictures of beautiful, perfect women, Karen decided to create these lovely ladies. During the process of putting likenesses of these less-than-perfect ladies on canvas, the ladies took on lives of their own and developed personalities.

Karen became a part of them, and they became a part of her. As a lady who has lived many years in the rugged mountains in a primitive cabin, she could relate to the rough lifestyle of these strong-willed ladies. When an art collector and friend asked for a little story for each "naughty lady," Karen already knew who these ladies were—their strengths and their weaknesses. She was instantly able to put together a life story for each of her ladies.

These naughty ladies have become an important part of our lives, and we hope they will become a part of your life too.

I am a believer. Karen really can turn anything into a piece of art, including all of the lives she touches.

Thank you, my lovely Dove.
Wayne-Bo

Acknowledgments

Thanks to the enterprising efforts of a few adventurous, spirited women, a much-needed service was provided for our forefathers, who settled the Wild West. As we applaud these men for their accomplishments, we should also include the women who brought a little joy and relief to an otherwise tough life, often devoid of comforts and kindness.

I would like to thank my wonderful parents, Bill and Bobbie Huffman, for sharing their special sense of humor that gets me through the tough times with a little comfort and sweetness.

A special thanks to my friends, Wayne Parks and Gary Cox, for their inspiration and encouragement. Also, many thanks to our mutual friend Rick Vredenburg, who brought us all together.

©Karen Carpenter '05

Introduction

The good Lord gave each of us many natural talents to work with in this life. We are all forced to trade those talents to make a livin. Now, who is to say which natural talents is more acceptable than others. As long as it don't take from another that which he don't wanta give, then it seems like God says, OK.

There's some Gents who say the Pearly Gates is the doorstep to Heaven, and my girls is heavenly angels. And then there's others who say it's the entrance into Hell. Seems to me that the Pearly Gates is home. When I'm standin at God's Pearly Gates, I hope that He don't judge as high-hatted as some of these ole biddies we got round here who ain't usin none of their natural talents fer the good of nobody. And they expect to make a livin at bein nasty and mean while everybody bends over backwards to take care of em.

If tradin my talents fer a livin makes me a whore, then I say we all have a little whorin in us. Maybe the real shame is in not usin yer natural talents to the good of nobody. If'n you ain't givin nothing in this world and yer only takin, yer missin half the picture. Yer missin the part that's gonna get you through the Pearly Gates and into Heaven. So give generously, Gents, and accept God's gifts graciously—and have a good time doin it.

Welcome to the Pearly Gates

Evenin Gents. Welcome to my "Pearly Gates." I'm the Belle of the balls, and this here is my ballroom, so let's dance.

If'n ya don't see what yer hanker'n for, jes jingle the Belle.

Things get a little heated up round here sometimes, so check yer shootin irons with Pete. You ain't gonna be needin um fer what yer hanker'n after. A whole arsenal ain't gonna protect you from a few little soiled doves.

Some fellas get to thinkin what they find here is love. Love don't live here, it jes comes and goes. All in all, ya cain't beat a sweet, soft woman when ya got a hanker'n.

My girls are all fine actresses. The way they act in bed should be entertainin at the least. How entertainin depends on how deep yer pockets are. My girls are such good actresses that you'd swear it was their first time and there won't never be another man as good as you, "Big Daddy."

There's some fine folks in town who seems to think that me and my girls ain't fit to live and work here. We ain't offerin up anything that ain't already been served up since the begininn of time, and the nice thing about my place is there's always plenty to go around with lots of leftovers the next day to stir into tomorrow's soup. If'n it weren't fer me and my girls, some of the men round here would be so cantankerous they couldn't even stand themselves much less each other. Women, on the other hand, seem to think they need a man with all his bad habits and will live with him for better or worse. Some Gents is only alive cause you can be hanged fer murder. The only way I'm willin to tolerate bad habits is if'n there's a profit and "fer better or worse" jest don't add up in my books.

So dig deep into them pockets, Gents, cause a man's worth ain't measured in inches. My girls jes love to see that ya have a real good time. They see men's hanker'ns as the original renewable resource jes waitin to be harnessed. As long as men can breath they'll be my favorite income source.

My girls are guaranteed to look better at night than by day. They look even better the more whiskey ya drink, and after a busy evenin of whoopin and holler'n you Gents begin thinkin they're good lookin and rich. That's the perfect combination fer beddin my girls. Jes make sure ya go home before the light of day—when last night's conquests become today's regrets.

I'd like you Gents to read my house rules posted over there on the wall. Fer you fellas who don't read or those who fergit easy, I'll run em down for you. Some of you boys been without a woman for so long ya forgot how to behave. Ya need to be reminded of the rules.

Pete, you may's well git these galoots another drink. This here is gonna be a rowdy night, I kin tell already.

As long as ya follow the rules, yer a welcomed guest, but fergit and yer outta here faster than you can lickety split.

Life ain't no piece of cake and I ain't yer cupcake. Any of the girls can be had if'n ya got the price, except the cook there. Leave my cook alone! Anyone knows it's jes plain foolish to mess with a cook. She's got a real unforgivin nature, and her ways of revenge makes us all shake in our boots.

House Rules

1. This here's my home not yers. Don't overstay yer welcome.

2. Stay as long as ya pay. It's a smart man who pays up front for what he wants behind.

3. Be good or be gone!

4. Drink all ya want as long as yer head is sittin' proud on yer shoulders and not in yer pants.

5. My girls ain't fer marryin till they's ready fer the pasture; till then they's mine.

6. Before partake'n in this feast fer sore eyes, remember, my girls have delicate noses, so buff yer buns.

7. Boots is made fer walkin, not layin. Keep em off my beds.

8. No gittin too pinchy. My girls don't like it. And I don't like it. Jes remember, these girls is my girls!

9. If'n ya spit on my floors, yer gonna be answerin to the Dragon Lady; and she favors torture fer a teacher. Her lessons are never forgotten.

10. Don't be so darned disgustin. Keep all body parts inside yer duds. No winkin willies. No full moons. Us ladies don't enjoy havin it wagged in our faces.

11. When you step out back to relieve yerself, stay outta Ting's garden. She goes crazy when her plants turn yellow. We don't understand what she's yellin, but every hog fer miles around knows his name is being called at the Pearly Gates.

12. If ya don't follow my rules, yer gonna be the only one sittin at the Pearly Gates in a wheelchair.

Now Gents, I'd like ya to see what's in my little chorus of Belle Ringers. The only bell ya ain't gonna be ringin at all is Liberty Belle, herself. I been rung so many times that there's a crack in the old Belle and the gap jes cain't be filled no more. That don't stop the old clapper from a-swingin a little once in a while, but I'm real choosy about who's doin the ringin. When I get a hanker'n I jes ring the ole dinner Belle to "come and git it," and Jake here is always ready with a good appetite. There ain't nothin wrong with a good appetite as long as ya eat at home. When I wanta let him know there's steak fer supper, I jes let him hear the sizzle.

I know that some of you fellas is so hanker'n that you'd mount a polecat, but they all done moved out cause they cain't stand the smell. With that kinda hanker'n ya ain't gonna be too choosy, but I'd like ya to know what yer gettin fer yer money. I'm right proud of my bevy of beauties. Each one is special and has her own unique talents, which come from years of trainin in the School of Hard Rocks. These girls don't know much about rockin cradles, but they can rock hard when they need to. Which is why I'm gonna give you their history—so you can choose yer own kinda rockin.

Chapter 1

Myrt and Gert

Myrt

Gert

Next on my program fer yer pleasure is a popular eastern sister act that I brought here fer yer on-stage entertainment. So keep yer hands off till they finish their performance, then it's on a first-come first-served basis and they're servin up a fine feast fer yer eyes. Now git yer hands outta yer pockets and put em together for the Boomer sisters, Myrt and Gert, and show em a fine welcome.

Myrt and Gert grew up in the streets of New York where their family landed when they come over on a ship from Ireland. There was no mistaking these bonny lassies' Irish background cause of their tempers. Their fiery natures are bound to give ya the fever. Their father left their mother to fend for herself while he headed for them thar hills of eastern Montana where gold was discovered. Their father, Kevin A. Boomer, was a "powder monkey" man and figured on workin the mines. Most people jes called him K.A., and he soon earned respect. K.A. Boomer, what a man he musta been.

Their mama never understood Papa's hanker'n fer the mines but that was all he knew, and New York was not the place fer a coal miner's son. Ma Boomer took in laundry to put her two girls through school, but all Myrt and Gert wanted to do was sing and dance. When they delivered Ma's clean laundry to the showgirls, they always lingered side stage to watch and learn. After years of watchin and practicin, they put together an act to take on the road. Their plan was to sing and dance their way West to find their daddy. They met a lot of "Sugar Daddys" waitin at the stage door but never did find Daddy. He had a pretty dangerous profession, so it probably shortened his life considerably.

Myrt and Gert Boomer are very talented ladies with varied abilities, and I betcha they'll dance their way right into yer hearts. Some ladies wear their hearts on their sleeves but that's too vulnerable for the Boomers. They wear their hearts on their backsides. Their mama advised them to jes sit tight on their hearts and save em fer a good man. That's jes what they been doin. They been sittin on their love so tight that over the years it's jes kinda fallen into the crack and its suckin the heart right out of em.

Lookin fer a good man is like tryin to blow smoke up a wildcat's arse. Still, the girls maintain a little bit of hope of findin Daddy, even if he falls short of their memory of the great K.A. As Gert says, "No man will ever be able to fill Daddy's boots, but they do fit Myrt. Myrt always did take after Daddy. She has that same explosive temper that always got him into trouble."

Myrt don't do too bad on the trouble side either. That's usually why the girls gotta move on to the next town. Myrt don't look fer trouble, it jes seems to find her. There ain't no man who could hold a match to Daddy (mainly because he always had gunpowder on him), and Myrt jes seems to rile up the men instead of sweet talkin em. Every word outta her mouth lets em know she ain't here to put up with their whinin. She says, "The only difference between a man and a pickle is that a man can fix a broke wagon wheel."

There are jes too many men and not enough good ones. The girls have traveled farther and wider than most of us, and on their journey they met lots of men who wanted to sample their obvious charms. Gert seems to be a more willin filly, and while Myrt seems to know all the wrong things to say, Gert knows all the right things to say. While Gert is sayin "Come on in," Myrt is sayin "Git on out." The Gents don't know if they's comin or goin, which is bad cause most Gents only know they're comin if their compass is pointin north and goin' if their south side's leavin out the door. Gert takes after her ma and has a real patient nature, maybe too patient. She jes puts up with that rude-man poop till finally Myrt gets a belly full and kicks arse. I once seen Myrt clear the whole house one night when she'd got about enough of those man ways.

Mostly, Myrt and Gert is a pair to draw to—a couple of queens who got no hope of findin their king and knowin fate dealt them a loosin hand. Good thing they got each other. They're still sittin' tight on their hearts, and they're still lookin to put a monkey into the act. Monkeys do everything a man can, and ya can teach em to roller skate.

Chapter 2

Muddy Mary

Muddy Mary

Muddy Mary ain't no pushover Gents,
but when push comes ta shove, she's a pro.

This lady is the one you Gents have been waitin fer all yer life. Meet Miss Muddy Mary. She is the delightful Miss that you love to watch every Wednesday night out back in the mud pits. We been holdin mud wrestlin matches every Wednesday night, and Mary is our featured wrestler. Course you Gents is more interested in watchin her dainties get all wet and muddy than paying mind to her holds. She challenges any man who is willin to git in the pit with her to go a round. Now, you tell me, who wouldn't want a go a round with Mary. There's even a prize for the man who can last the longest, not that there even needs to be a prize. There's great fun for the spectators with shoutin and bettin, but it always ends in Mary on top and the looser grinnin from ear to ear. I always like to see a good loser, but then losin is sometimes winnin with an opponent like Mary.

Mary came from a local family who had way too many kids. Mama jes kept havin babies, and Papa was hopin fer as many farm hands as he could git. Them people never did figure out what they were doin to deserve all them farm hands. Them boys all grew up as lazy as Papa, so fer all their efforts they still don't have no help with the chores. They jes got a lot of mouths to feed. They's all slackers 'cept Mary. She's the only girl but Mama in the family, so she had to learn to wrestle jes to survive.

We all take the gifts the good Lord gives us to git along, and Mary's gifts began to show themselves one day when the town was flooded from a heavy rain and gettin around was a humblin experience. The buggys and wagons were dry-docked, and the horses all had very nasty tempers. It was lookin like business was gonna be slow fer a few days so Mary went fer a walk. She was broke when she left, but when she came back her purse was as full of money as her boots were of mud. She was plum covered in mud, head to toe, and mad as a cornered wolverine.

That was one woman with attitude. She told us how she stepped off the boardwalk to cross over to the Pearly Gates and sunk into the mud. Her boots filled up with the stuff and when she tried to move out of the way of a passin freight wagon, she found herself stuck fast in the muck of the town streets. Spring round here jes seems to bring out all the water from the winter meltdown and leaves it all in the middle of the road.

Mary don't do well with mucky middle of the road situations and tends to deal with it like stompin snakes. It was an attitude she picked up while growing up with all them brothers. So naturally, when them old cowhands started whoopin and hollerin bout this little wet hen bein stuck in the barnyard muck, she stepped right outta them boots—ready to do battle.

First up was old Stinky McGinty, who was down before he even got started. Then came Willy B. who fancied himself to be the toughest hand in Montana, but he was no match fer Mary. By this time, the crowd was beginning to gather, and some was even makin bets. My bar was real busy with all them dry-throated warblers out front poppin in fer refreshments.

Them Gents was so starved fer something to break the cabin fever of winter blues, they spent a good part of what they dug outta the ground all winter in jes one day.

I'd never seen anybody get so mad over a little mud, but Mary seemed to love it in a kinda strange way. Mud is definitely Mary's element, and she felt right at home. When a sister goes toe to toe with a brother in the muck, she has to get a little dirty to get to the Pearly Gates.

Mary busted the gates right down gettin through. She left a trail of muck all the way up the stairs and into her room. We followed the trail to the closed door, but decided we better leave her alone.

It took us three days to begin talkin to her. We jes slid the food under the door for her. Once she could tell us what had happened and how she'd got all that money, we all started gettin an idea of how to boost business on Wednesday nights. The morale of all the Gents is so low in the middle of the week that they don't come around. We started, "Wednesday Night Mud Wrestling." "Bring Yer Money Boys—All Challenges Welcome."

These boys 'round here love Mary cause she's the only woman they can whup up on and she whups right back. They love to lose, and the whoopin and holler'n makes it even better. The madder Mary gets, the more the crowd cheers.

Mary learned fightin at home, and it's jes the only way she knows to deal with a man. Her mama had to learn it to keep Papa off her, and Mary learned from Mama how to keep her brothers off. Fightin Mama always said, "Keep em on their backs, Mary. They's more humble that way."

My idea was to make money off Mary's rage. I don't quite understand why men seem to get big laughs outta see'n us ladies get mad. I guess maybe men know how ornery they are to women, and they like to see justice happen to the other guy. What's so funny 'bout see'n a woman goin beserk on a man and then takin bets on how long it's gonna take? That's even stranger. But who am I to argue over success. Mary gets her revenge on men. Men get relief from their boredom and get punished for any sins they wanta commit. And little ole me jes gets richer. What a great little town we live in. Everybody's happy.

Chapter 3

Miss Goldie

Goldie

Goldie, known by the miners as "Golden Nuggets"
can give ya the fever fer sure.

Now Gentlemen, I would like you to feast yer sore eyeballs on the lovely Miss Goldie, who is no stranger to you miners. You probably remember her from when she was workin the miners in the field. That's where she got her name "Gold Nugget" or Goldie as we know her. She got her name from what she charged fer services rendered. Big nugs or small nugs, she serviced em all.

Goldie started out marryin her childhood sweetheart when she was jes barely a woman, and the two of em decided to get their brand new start out West. They had a little money that Goldie's father gave em fer gettin hitched, so they bought an old wagon, a team of oxen, and a milk cow. Goldie had her hope chest full of linens that she had been collectin since she was jes a little lady. She was given a beautiful chest but it was empty. She hoped for a chest that was full and voluptuous so the men would love her. That was the best advice her mama could give Goldie, "Grow up and develop a full and voluptuous bosom. All your problems are solved if'n you got a full

and voluptuous bosom." Hah! I got yer full and voluptuous bosom and it never brought me nothing but a pain
in the neck and fallen arches from standin and restin
these bosoms on the bar. Nowadays it seems to be the
only way to get cleavage!

Well, as you see, Goldie never did develop what she was
hoping fer in her chest. She did develop a talent fer sewin
a fine stitch. She makes the loveliest gowns and hats you
ever seen. But—back to my story, before Goldie's chest
got ravaged and all her linens scattered to the wind.

Goldie and her young man set out fer Montana after
hearin about the gold bein discovered there. By the time
they spent a couple of months on the trail, they had run
outta jes about everythin and still had another month to
go, and it was the hottest and most dangerous month of
all. They was so young they was cheated outta every
penny they had, and then one night them Injuns raided
their camp and left em both fer dead. They didn't even
steal the old nag that was all Goldie had left to her. When
she recovered, she took stock of her assets and found that
them Injuns had taken full advantage of her assets while
she was fainted.

Goldie recovered enough to ride that old nag into a
minin' camp where the kindness of the men there was
overwhelmin. This mining camp had about two hundred
men and one other woman, who did all the laundry and
cookin, ole Black Hettie. Hettie came from somewhere
down South where they do something called voodoo. She
found a way to make Goldie believe that she had full,
voluptuous bosoms. It made Goldie think she had some

special power over men that made em love her and give her special gifts and gold—lots of gold.

Course, soon Gold Nugget earned a fortune in gold usin a much easier method than those miners was usin. Goldie was an enterprizin young woman. She jes wasn't good at managerin her riches or her love life. She was lookin fer what she had lost to them Injuns.

When she left all the boys in the gold fields it was like the gold had left the sunrise and the sunset, and everything in between was jes plain dirt. There was "gold in them thar hills," but no more. Goldie needed a change. You can get too much of a good thing. When ya got special powers over men like Goldie has, you realize one day that all that lovin is getting old. Cold facts begin creepin into the picture. The mirror becomes too brutally truthful. It screams, "Flat!" All those voodoo illusions are jes a lotta hooey and lovin like that jes makes callouses.

Miss Goldie came to the Pearly Gates cause she was ready to settle down. All that travelin was wearing on her, not to mention all that attention. Goldie took a shine to all my girls here, and she liked havin a family fer a change.

It's good to have someone at yer back in this business. Goldie needed some protection cause she was always ready to marry the first man what came along jes so she'd have someone to help her protect all of her gold. We talked her into puttin it in the bank for security instead of makin a mistake with a man she knew nothin about. She no sooner put it in the bank than the bank was robbed.

They stole everything and wiped out Goldie's savings. Banks ain't much more secure than a man.

We all helped her drink her sorrows away that night but come the light of day, waking up with a horrible hangover, she was hit with cold reality. Start all over again! There ain't nothin fair 'bout life.

Goldie is now one of my angels and is ringin bells every night at the Pearly Gates. The men jes love this light-hearted dove, whose long legs is better at wrappin around than at runnin. She still collects plenty of nuggets, but the job isn't 24 hours a day.

She can take better care of herself cause I instruct my girls in the fine art of bein smart. It ain't something that comes natural to women, cause mostly men don't want us that way. If'n we was smart, we couldn't be talked into half the stuff we go fer. Just cause we fall fer a bunch of horse dooky way too often don't mean we're stupid. It jes means we're gettin smarter. Jes think about it, Gents. If'n I can stay healthy and live a long life, I'm gonna pass you all up and someday I'm gonna be runnin things. You boys should be worried, cause with me in charge, your gonna spend old age in hell—Belle's Hell.

Course, yer already in Belle's Hell, and I don't see nobody complainin. I'm smart enough to make hell feel good.

When Goldie joined my doves, she became a partner in our Union of Professional Shady Ladies. We have many businesses cause we have so much talent among us. We take care of each other and everyone who works fer us. You might say we got eyes and ears jes about everywhere in town. We know everything that's goin on round here. We don't tell, but we do take good advantage of a bad situation.

One of our investments is our own retirement ranch, the Wild Horze Ranch. We all have a plan to get outta this business here cause we know all too well that youth is a fleeting condition: when you figure out the right way to use it, it's time to give it up. Youth jes wasn't meant to be used forever. That's too dangerous. Youth is all velocity and no direction, so they spin in decreasing circles til they fly up their own arses.

When we soiled doves retire, we want to live well and never have to bed another bugger again. The only studs we're gonna bed is putting the livestock in the barn.

This here is the Pearly Gates to our Heaven, which is the Wild Horze Ranch. We "angels of the gates" is wide open fer business, Gents. Anything you want, anyway you want it.

Chapter 4

Miss Sophie

Sophie

Sophie handles Gents as well as her mules.
Jes don't git her riled up.

ow dear hearts, you have the pleasure of meetin the one and only Miss Sophie. Miss Sophie is a favorite of the cowboys. I guess maybe she jes has that certain smell they get used to.

Sophie grew up lovin horse flesh. Her papa was a blacksmith, and she would help out sometimes with the four-legged tenants. Sometimes Papa would let her test ride a horse he'd jes shoed. Sophie was her papa's little girl and the apple of his eye. Sophie loved her papa, and long after that horse kicked him in the head, Sophie tried to keep the smithy shop goin. But it was jes too much work fer a pretty little thing like Sophie.

Sophie had the nature of a muleskinner and could use that whip of hers as good as any man I ever saw. I think that's part of her charm. To some Gents, it's the thrill of thinkin any minute she might take out her whip, and, if she's in the right mood, she might scare the hide right off ya. I hear from some of the Gents that she's pretty excitin.

Sophie relates equally well to mules and men. "They's both a lot alike—stubborn. They only see one way—their way."

Sophie says, "Sometimes the only way to reason with em is to get out the ole whip. It opens up a mind real fast and makes fer right agreeable critters. Otherwise, a gal can waste a lot of time tryin to sweet talk em into doin what they know they oughta be doin. Sometimes they's stubborn jes cause they wanta be whipped. Maybe, when ya been out on the range drivin cattle all day, ya loose all yer feelin and bein whipped can be good if it brings back the feelin."

Feelins is funny things. Even though we know we can get hurt, we still go fer it cause the alternatives are so borin. If'n yer bored with life, it's cause you ain't doin. Have you checked lately, Gents? Maybe yer dead. After all, you are standin at the Pearly Gates!

Sophie sure has a way with critters, four-legged and two-legged. Some of these studs that come in here struttin their manly charms jes deserve to run into Sophie. She jes bites em on the ear to let em know that she's boss. Then she takes em on her own little cattle drive. It don't matter so much how long a ride ya have as how well ya ride it. There's more to ridin than jes sittin in the saddle and danglin yer feet. Ride em Sophie!

When a cowboy tells ya he wants to ride behind, ya better find out whose behind cause he probably ain't talkin about no horse ride. Cowpokes been waltzin those bovines all the way from Texas and by the time they get em to market and get paid, dancin is the last thing on their minds. They hear the ole cowbell janglin for them, and Sophie is their favorite Belle Ringer.

Sophie has a slick way of dealin with the ornery ones— jes throw em down and dig yer heels in on the big ones, and catch the little ones around the neck. For those smart-ass ones who jes don't fit in a saddle, they jes ain't even worth gettin' emotional about.

Miss Sophie's the one who gave us the idea for the Wild Horze Ranch. She jes has a hanker'n to raise horses. The more men she deals with, the more she loves them horses. She never fergot the things her daddy taught her. "Never put up with an ornery horse, jes shoot em. If'n they won't listen to the whip, then they ain't fer no good. Shoot em. Horses is jes like men, if'n they don't make money, get rid of em."

Sophie never found a man as good as Papa. She never did understand her Mama, who took off with a gamblin man headed fer San Francisco. Papa jes weren't exciting enough fer her. After Mama left, Sophie became Papa's whole life. All he could give Sophie was his knowledge of horses. Sophie wants to use her natural-born talents to breed horses instead of men. Most men is jes too ornery to use a whip on, so Papa's advice was ta shoot them too, but you can be hanged fer that even if the world would be better off minus a few ornery critters.

When Sophie straps on her chaps, you know she's gonna be doin some ridin, and if she's carryin her whip,

you know she's planning on gettin someone's attention—
and he better be doin some listenin. When she rides, she
likes to get real personal with the critter. It's better fer
control, and Sophie likes to be in control. Horses ain't
quite as stubborn as men, so when Sophie retires at the
ranch, life will be much easier. That's Sophie's idea of
heaven on earth, the Wild Horze Ranch.

Chapter 5

Pokesalotus

"The Princess," as we call her, can ride like the wind fer all them warrior spirits.

Pokesalotus here is our own little bit of royalty. She was dumped at the Pearly Gates by a real gnarley lookin character who wasn't lookin to get hitched. He dumped and ran. I shore didn't know what I was goin to do with this little soiled dove who looked like she could take flight at the drop of yer hat.

After some pretty rough days of stumbling through talking, we finally understood why she looked so wild.

It seems her people were mostly all killed off in a raid by soldiers with a rage burnin in em and whiskey fannin the flame. There oughta be a law against that! Some folks seems to think they got more rights to be here than others, and they git real uppity about it. Course, when they's six feet under, they all rot about the same and who knows what happens to their souls. I bet God don't allow no firearms at his Pearly Gates neither. He'd jes hafta boot em to Hell where they kin kill off each other forever. I wonder where they go when the Devil gives em the boot.

39

I do think some of them fellers been passin through the Pearly Gates here on earth.

I could see this little dove was in bad need of a helping hand, but I could also see she had the same assets as all the rest of us girls. She jes needed to wrap em up in some fancy lace and ribbons to make the Gents take notice. We finally talked her outta them smelly ole buckskins and into a tub of hot water. Three hours, a bar of lye soap, and one of Gert's fancy hairdos topped off with one of Mary's clean dresses later, we had ourselves a first rate "Indian Princess."

It turns out that we didn't need to teach the Princess a thing. She was a natural. Her main problem was the springs in the bed. She jes couldn't git used to "bounce-back." She claimed it had more bounce than a wild horse that don't want tamin. Bein the smart girl she was, she soon learned to use the bounce-back to make her work easier. With the right rhythm she could make those springs sing.

A lot of men have a taste fer royalty so they can feel like a King! The Princess became real popular and soon came to be known as "Princess Pokesalotus."

The thing with the Princess is that she ain't jes royalty, she works like a commoner, sweatin with the best of us. That energy of hers is from all the grudges she has fer them "crazy whitemen" and her way of gettin back is to ride em hard and take the only thing that means anything to em—money—and she takes plenty of that.

Pokesalotus is planning on raisin the best and the biggest herd of horses in all of Montana at the Wild Horze Ranch. She also hopes fer a handsome brave to come ridin up on a white stallion and sweep her up in his strong arms and take her to his teepee as his woman. Now, don't that sound familiar. All us girls know that dream. Hope, like beds, springs eternal. And jes like beds, hopes have their ups and downs, which after a while of goin up and down get pretty loosened up and worn down. Course, like beds, the bounce-backs get slower with age. Too many bounce-backs takes its toll on the old body.

When Pokesalotus was a young'un, her people lived on and with all the land round here. Her people were happy and content. Life was simple. Then it got really mixed up when the whiteman came into their land. All Pokey wanted to do was ride horses. She would sneak one of her father's horses and ride with the wind. She was better than all the boys who were always practicing their warrior skills.

Pokey wanted to be a warrior, but she was born a woman. The boys grew up to be warriors. They were fierce warriors, but all either died fightin or were sent, broken, to the reservation. Pokey escaped on foot like a woman. She wandered for a long time jes surviving off what the Mother Earth could offer. That's what she was doin when ole Salty Peters found her livin in a cave. She shared her vittles with him, and after that they were jes together. But ole Salty was not one to hook up with nobody fer very long. He liked his loneliness.

Pokey had spent enough years alone. She wanted some companionship. She really missed her mother and sisters. Women need other women. So, one particularly nasty, stormy night, ole Salty paid the Pearly Gates a visit with our beloved Pokey in tow. He talked me into takin Pokey in as one of my girls. I was reluctant at first, cause she looked like hell, but I knew that all of us girls look pretty bad when we're jes out there surviving.

Pokesalotus is left to carry on the traditions. Now she rides like a warrior and counts many coup. A buck fer a buck. Pokesalotus is truly a warrior in my book.

Chapter 6

Mae Bea Laid

Mae Bea Laid

This poor child of misfortune may never know that

it's the name that's ta blame.

Yer gonna love this sweet, rosy-cheeked lass, Gents. This little lady suffers from a name her ma and pa cursed her with. She was named after her two grandmothers, who were both very happy with their namesake; but the combination of the two names brought my little Mae Bea nothing but trouble till she came here to the Pearly Gates.

My Mae just never seems to be certain about anything, and men always take her name to be a yes. Sometimes a person needs to say "no," and "maybe" jes opens the door to the folks who know how to rob the fruit from the tree. Miss Mae Bea was a peach, ripe fer the pickin, and that salesman knew it.

Mae Bea was the youngest of five children, and Mama Laid jes couldn't handle the farmin way of life. She jes kept havin babies, and her good looks was slippin away. She saw herself dryin up like an old plum in the sun. One day she jes wasn't there anymore, and five young'uns was more than Papa Laid could handle. He was way too busy with raisin his crops to be raisin children, so they all grew up fendin fer themselves.

Mae was a quiet little creature who mostly jes hid behind the stove playin with some mangy old pup. Nobody paid any attention to little Mae cause they all had chores. Then one day a travelin salesman came to the door when everybody but Mae was out in the field. That smooth-talking dude was jes looking fer a soft touch. He traded Mae a fancy pair of black French silk stockins fer her virtue. Mae was way too young to know the value of such a thing, and once it was gone she couldn't get it back. Her fifteen years of sittin behind the stove jes hadn't prepared her fer what life had in store. Mae Bea had learned, in her quiet little world, that she could answer jes about all questions by sayin her name, Mae Bea.

Mama Laid always told Mae that if she was ever at a loss fer words, she should jes call on her Grandmother Spirits, and they would protect her. She never understood why sayin her grandmas' names brought her so many strange experiences instead of savin her. She kept thinking that the Grandma Spirits were givin her good guidance, but maybe not.

When that salesman got ready to leave, he asked Mae if'n she wanted to come along fer a while, and Mae Bea answered "Mae Bea" with that charmin little smile peekin out from behind a shoulder. Mae put on her stockins and has been wearin them ever since. They're a good reminder of her lost virtue.

I bet you Gents is wonderin how Mae Bea came to the Pearly Gates. Well, ya see, that same sales dude came here, and he tried to sell me this sweet peach; but I squashed that fruit picker, took his peach, and sent him packin.

He left Mae with another reminder of her lost virtue. You see, Mae was left with a baby in the makin, and she had no idea what she was in fer. She had to grow up fast, cause that baby wasn't gonna wait fer her to grow up like usual. He came three months later in the middle of a snowstorm. We had to get ole Doc Leecher out in the night and little Iffy came into this world about as good as it gets for a guy—in a feather bed surrounded by fallen angels jes awaitin their turn to hold the littlest angel. There's some folks who would say that the Pearly Gates is no proper place to bring up a child, but little Iffy gits more than his fair share of love; and when he becomes a man he'll know jes how to please a woman fer sure. That puts him way ahead of most men, cause mostly women is jes a mystery to em.

I think, maybe figurin out women is men's biggest battle. Men can fight bloody wars, conquer nations, overcome huge obstacles in their careers; they can move mountains, but when it comes to facin a little blue-eyed, delicate lady, they fall to pieces. All of a sudden this confident, ornery ole bugger cain't even speak his own name much less get up the nerve to ask fer a kiss. No wonder it's so hard to get lucky.

I train my girls to make talkin easy fer a man, cause they have too much trouble with it. You'd think words would come easy to em cause they don't hold back when they're barkin out orders. Some men, like Mae's travelin salesman, think that fast talking women is the best way. Jes tell em what they wanta hear and get em into the hay. Take what you want and leave em worn out and cryin. There ain't much to be proud of there.

Little girls come outta the womb talkin, but fer boys, they jes don't seem to get it. They can sure yell though; that seems to come natural. Little Iffy had a fine set of lungs and didn't hesitate to use em. We have to keep the little nipper quiet when the Gents is here cause they don't want a reminder of what their pleasure can leave behind. It scares em so bad they fergit what they're here fer.

Someday, maybe Mae will find little Iffy a daddy; but until that day, he's got about everything he needs right here. Havin no daddy is better than havin one who don't want nothing to do with a young'un. Life is hard and men get jes as hard tryin to live it. They don't want to have to take care of nothin except themselves (and most don't do a good job of that). Takin on a woman and young'uns is about the hardest thing a man can do. Some are crazy enough to take it on outta choice, and some have it forced on em, but either way, I got respect fer the Gent who steps up to the task and sees it through to the end. Respect is something we all want, but very few wanta earn it. Mostly, it's something you earn by givin, cause when you hafta give respect, you learn what it's all about. By the time you spend a lifetime respectin others, you realize you get what you give—no more, no less.

Now, on to my next Belle Ringer.

Chapter 7

Fifi la Toosh

*Fifi is our pride and joy. She's our Nymph du Prairie,
imported straight from France.*

Okay, Fifi, it's yer turn. Gents, this little lady with a big heart is Miss Fifi La Toosh. I jes hafta caution you about Fifi; she's a bit small, but so's dynamite. And we all know what a wallop that packs. Fifi's height puts her in a very dangerous position for you Gents, so guard yer jewels. If she goes off on you, jes sit on her and ride out the storm.

When yer small, like Fifi, you learn to fight fer everthing you get. Fifi was born in Paris, France, to a can-can mama at the Moulin Rouge. Her papa was a man of the arts and liked hangin round the dancehall dollies. Like so many artists, he earned a few side bucks paintin scenery on stages while waitin to be discovered. Paintin scenes at rehearsals put him in a good place to work on his favorite hobby, pinchin tooshes. He could pinch a lot of toosh when they all lined up and flipped their skirts over their heads, and Papa was jes the right height. He was a man who knew his limits and put em to good use. Everybody has something that ain't quite right about em. You jes gotta learn to use what you got.

Fifi is our very own "Nymph du Prairie." Everything she has is pure French, and I'm sure you Gents know what that means, don't ya. She never speaks in nothin but French, but when she lets loose on ya, you'll understand perfectly.

Fifi's mama always told her that "special things come in small packages, like diamonds." Her mama always had lots of Gents hangin round the back door with lots of pretty presents. The small ones were her favorites. She would cuddle Fifi in her lap and tell her she was her favorite "small package" and that her heart was a perfect diamond. Diamonds are real sparkley, but they're also cold and hard, which is a perfect description of what our Fifi grew up to be. Fire and ice, that's Fifi.

Here at the Pearly Gates we like to dress Fifi up in a fancy little weddin dress and get her to pop outta a fake weddin cake. Then all the Gents fight to see who's goin on the honeymoon. I hear tell that she truly is special and that she has learned to use her talents in ways they never saw before—or even thought of in their wildest dreams.

Fifi is the Queen of my little coop of doves. When she came to the Pearly Gates it was in a fine carriage pulled by a couple of fine, white horses and driven by her "man" (Fifi never treated him very good so he took off). Fifi ain't much fer lovin nobody but herself. To Fifi, Gents is jes fer usin and losin. When she's through with em, she jes casts em aside and makes room fer the next. They always need to give her plenty of gifts, cause that's what she's used to. I ain't never seen one little woman command so much attention from so many Gents. But, I guess size don't matter, does it fellas?

Fifi has found a way of turnin a handicap into a special talent. Some folks might whine about all their hardships, but not Fifi. She knows that she is special cause she's small, and she thinks everybody has somethin special about em. They jes need the chance to show it. Each night she has a special Gent and spends the whole night jes showin him how special he is. No wonder she has such generous grooms fer her bride act.

They're usually kinda broken up a bit, but nursing them back to health is part of the special treatment that Fifi provides. By now you can bet she's right good with bandages and tinctures. By the time she gets a Gent all wiped off and bandaged up, he fergets all about hurtin and recovery is on its way. One night with Fifi can last a lifetime in yer memories, and its good fer at least a year's worth of dreams. She makes so much off of jes one Gent that she's a one-hump-a-nighter.

What a gifted lady that woman is. There's nobody can hold a candle to Fifi when it comes to telling stories. When things get slow round here, Fifi keeps us all laughin and sometimes even sheddin a tear or two with her stories. She's a real knee-slapper. Jes make sure Fifi ain't sittin on yer lap when ya slap yer knee.

Fifi don't take kindly to slappin less she's doin the slappin. Mostly though, she ain't got time fer that. If she don't like ya, it's the icy treatment that'll get ya.

Even though Fifi has many Gents who wanta take care of her, she don't wanta be owned like some trained monkey. She ain't no organ grinder's monkey pet. I think that would make anybody cold-hearted. Nobody likes to do tricks fer treats, but we all do it and we use whatever talents we have to get us there. When you kin use yer talents as well as Fifi, you minimize yer tricks and maximize yer treats. That sounds pretty good to an old "slapper" like me.

Chapter 8

Miss Violet

Violet

Shrinking Violet has a way of smiling that makes Gents wanta take care of her.

Now, Gents, to tell you about this sweet little wisp of a willow, I gotta talk real quiet cause that's jes how Violet is. Miss Violet is as delicate as the flower she was named after. As tiny and vulnerable as she looks, she is also persistent. I seen violets growin right outta the rocks where I didn't think anything could survive, much less a frail tiny blossom. Miss Violet always seems to come through in a pinch. In fact, she kinda likes to be pinched if'n you know what I mean.

I'll take a moment here, Gents, to caution you about gettin too pinchy. Violet is one of my girls. Don't make me get rough. It takes too much outta me, besides ruinin my manicure.

Miss Violet musta had something pretty bad happen to her, cause she sure don't wanta be anywhere.

All I know about Violet's past is what I get outta listenin to her sleep talkin. She's got some bad dreams in her sometimes, but mostly that's jes when her tonic is wearin off. She's got a hanker'n fer that tonic that's like a two-headed snake. It goes in two opposite directions at once. That's why she sleeps so much; she's tired from the struggle of havin direction but not knowin which way to go to get there. And that's why she ain't goin nowhere. It's a lot easier to jes sleep and dream—that don't take no direction at all. Violet dreams of blue skies, rainbows, and fields of daisies.

Violet came to the Pearly Gates by way of a buzzard that was passin through our town. He was gettin rich off sellin miners snake oil to relieve the aches and pains from too much work and too little pleasure. It didn't seem to help the pain much, but it made em not care about nothing except gettin more snake oil. Violet was another cure-all that buzzard was sellin. I jes couldn't stand seein the damage that creep was doin. I jes had to arrange fer some of the boys to run that sucker outta town. He was wearin nothing but some very chic tar and feathers when he left. I think he looked better as a bird than a poor excuse fer a man. That ole buzzard flew the coop and left me with a new fallen dove fer my little family.

"Pete, I think Violet needs to see old Doc Leecher again. She keeps gettin farther and farther away, but she still ain't goin nowhere. I don't know what she's dreamin of, but it must be good cause she's smilin."

"Violet, honey, wake up. Violet. Violet!"

"Pete, maybe you need to help Violet to her room fer a little nap and make sure she don't take no more 'Pretty Pills' cause she's pretty enough."

In fact, she got so pretty she went right over the edge of pretty. She likes dancin on the edge. She keeps the Gents on the edge too, and some of em likes it.

Violet's got a good return clientele cause those Gents jes wanta see her when she's so happy. They keep hopin she'll let them be the one who makes her smile. We sportin ladies like to keep you Gents smiling, and we know jes how to do it.

Sometimes a pat on the head and a scratch on the behind is jes what some of you old dogs need. Cowboys kinda like gettin a full belly, and good ole boys likes jes sittin and talking on the porch in the evening sunset.

Violet is out of the runnin fer the night. Violets don't last long, you know. You gotta jes enjoy em where they bloom and hope to see em smile when they're awake. It's always such a joy to see em bloom each spring. Hope is like spring—fresh and new and there is always tomorrow. So, if'n you hanker fer Violet, Gents, you'll hafta come back tomorrow cause she's feelin as wilted as summer's last violet.

Chapter 9

One-Legged Effie

@Karen Carpenter 05

Elvis

Ever since ole Snake Oil Lenny sold our Effie
that remedy, she's been feelin no pain.

I jes know you Gents are goin to enjoy the next easy lady of lost virtue. She is our own One-Legged Effie, who come to us from the stockyards in Kansas. She was bred on a cattle ranch and had no taste fer the bovines in her future. Her tastes ran more to the cowhands a-sittin their horses. She wanted to be mounted, and that was all that was on her mind when she turned sweet sixteen. She had no mama to teach her the more refined qualities of bein a lady. Her mama run off with one of the hands shortly after Effie was born, leavin behind Effie and three older brothers. Course, Effie, bein a baby with no one but brothers to raise her, grew up rough. She was surrounded by men and never knew how to be a woman. She sure learned what men like, and once she figured out that she was different from them, she saw how she could be very popular. She had those cowhands spendin all their wages on pretty things fer Effie.

Effie was the best ride on the ranch. She had them boys fightin fer her favors, and it got so bad that her Daddy had to send her away to a religious girls' school to get refinement (and so's he could get some work outta them hands).

Effie didn't make it long in the school. She soon learned that virtue was its own punishment. Life jes weren't worth livin without a cowpoke once in a while. Effie yearned fer a roll in the hay. She jes couldn't deal with them ladies of the Lord. She craved the sweet smell of cowboys, horses, and barns. She decided to run off with the first cowpoke she got wind of. The Sisters of Mercy hired a young buck to mend fences. He was jes passin through on his way to Montana. Amos was pursuin dreams of his own spread, and Effie thought Montana sounded like a place with lots of men jes like home. She paid him to take her along.

There's all kinds of snakes in the world. There's the kind that tempt a pretty lady, and there's the kind with rattles on their tails. Effie was used to temptation. She didn't fight it; she jes went with it and enjoyed it. She learned at that school that it is jes too hard to fight that which comes natural.

Handlin cowpokes came natural to Effie; it was the other kind of snake that got her leg.

Those creepy critters; I hate em. The one that snuck up on Effie lived jes long enough to regret bitin her. Effie picked that ole snake up by the tail and used it like a whip. Popped that sucker's head clean off. That bite on the leg caused Effie to hafta lay over fer the winter. She got a room at a female boardin house, and the sisters there taught Effie how to make a livin at what she liked doin fer fun. She was a natural. That leg of hers gave her fits though. It jes wouldn't heal up right, so the Doc had to chop it off at the knee. Effie walked in circles fer a while til she learned how to use a cane to go forward. Once she got the hang of it, she took off fer Montana.

Effie decided she needed a husband, so she went to an agency and got herself a mail-order husband. Sure nuf, there was a good soundin man jes pine'n fer the likes of Effie. He wrote that he had a spread of his own, and he sent her money for the train trip. Effie needed a new life, and a train ride was jes right fer a "grand lady" to meet her new husband.

So, with a fine new dress and hat, she set out fer Montana. Effie arrived with more money than she'd left with. That one leg don't slow her down one bit, exceptin when she wants to get caught.

When Effie arrived, there was no husband to meet her, jes an old undertaker with his hand out fer the price of a pine box. It seems Effie was a bride and a widow in one day, which made her nothing 'cept lonely and broke. She shoulda asked about the size of ole Joe's spread, cause it turned out that it was nothing more than a shack out back of the saloon.

Effie went back to the only trade she knew and put that little shack to good use. There was many a night that ole roof was hoppin right up off that shack like the lid on a teakettle blowin steam.

Now, I don't wanta be ringin my own bell, but I got the best house in all of Montana and my sweet little Belle Ringers are known far and wide fer their performance. One-Legged Effie heard about my Ringers and decided to go from the "crib" to a real brass bed in my house. Now she's makin those bedsprings ring with what sounds like music to my ears.

Chapter 10

Ting-A-Ling

@Karen Carpenter 05

Ting comes with a warning label.
Don't git on her bad side, or you'll meet the
Dragon Lady.

This here lady is not one of my girls. This is Ting-A-Ling, and she keeps this old cracked bell swingin high. I couldn't do without her.

Ting showed up at the Pearly Gates outta nowhere. She was jes there with her strange little bag in one hand and her umbrella in the other—standin in the doorway, drippin wet. She couldn't have weighted more than 90 pounds. That bag of hers has always been a mystery, cause it seems like everything that's needed here comes outta that bag.

Ting moved right in and took over. She does all the cookin, cleanin, and washin up around here, but even better, she keeps us well with her magic potions. She's got a potion for everything. Even the Indian medicine man sometimes comes to the back door and Ting slips him a little bottle or bag of somethin.

When Ting cooks, you never know what yer gittin. We all jes quit askin and jes eat what she serves up. When Ting rings the ole dinner bell at the Pearly Gates, she uses a large gong that makes you wanta duck and cover. She may be tryin to warn us. It's pretty suspicious when she serves each person at the table a little different meal. She says, "Everybody different—get different food—depends on how they think. Some people naturally stupid. You people here stupid to start with and you work hard at bein more stupid. So hard, you forgot that smart ever existed."

When Ting sings, I listen hard. It seems to take me a long time to finally get what she's sayin, and then I realize I already knew it and I wasted all that time tryin to understand something I already knew. Boy, these inscrutable Chinese ain't to be messed with. I'm thinking maybe they're smarter or something.

Ting is most proud of her garden, so Gents, when yer stumbling round out back, you best stay a long ways away from them pretty flowers. Just like them flowers, Ting can pack a wallop if'n you don't respect her.

As Ting always says, "You people crazy."

She says that we kill ourselves tryin to be happy when if'n we'd jes slow down and take a look, we might see that we're already happy doin what we're doin. Some folks might see they're unhappy and they enjoy bein that way. So, why kill yerself when yer havin so much fun tryin to be happy. If'n you ain't happy doin what yer doin, then do somethin else.

I guess I'm happy to jes be tryin. I'll try anything once, twice if'n it don't kill me, and after that it jes might become a hit.

Ting is our mama round here, and she calls us girls "Hells Belles." Hells Belles ring every night at the Pearly Gates, but the good Lord don't seem to listen to all the jingle-jangle. He knows it's jes us crazy people tryin hard to be happy and if'n he jes leaves us to dance at the "Gate," we'll eventually get tired and settle down. I sure hope the good Lord is right, cause I'm gettin tired of dancin.

Chapter 11

Liberty Belle

Liberty Belle

Some of you Gents have asked me how the hell did I get here. Well, that there is a mighty long story, and I think I better make it short cause I kin see from the way yer hats is hangin on yer laps that there's more pressin things on yer minds. I'll tell it short and sweet boys, so hang on to yer hats with both hands.

"Little Belly," as Mama called me, was a coddled little dove from the git-go. Mama always had lots of sisters all livin together in her house, and there were lots of Uncles who came and went. They always brought pretty presents.

All my Uncles wanted to see me dance while they waited for Mama or my Aunties. They would cheer and clap to see me wiggle my belly, so that was how I got my name, Belly. From there it got changed to Belle when I grew up and found that the Gents would cheer when I wiggled any part of me, not jes my belly. I been the "Belle of Balls" for most of my life.

I have no idea who my Daddy was and never had no need fer one. Mama always said that she jes hoped he was one of the smart, handsome ones.

My mama was all I needed. Everybody loved my mama. Mama had stupid down to a fine art, but she totally knew how to make stupid fun and everybody wanted to be a part of whatever she had goin. When she was gone from my life, I felt like the rug got pulled out from under me. Fortunately, one of Mama's regular Gents was a lawyer, and Mama had taken care of her Little Belly in her will. I inherited this place here. Mama always said, "I'll meet you at the Pearly Gates someday Belly." There is a little part of Mama in all of us Deservin Angels dancin here at the Gates.

It seems that Mama had entered into a business venture with one of her Gents who visited regular from out West. He had always hoped that Mama would bring her girls to his town cause there was lots a ornery fellas who needed the refinement that Mama's girls could provide. Mama jes didn't have the urge to travel, but she had a good business sense cause, when gold was discovered, that town got really wild. When Mama died, I had the travelin urge so I took the tools of the trade that Mama had passed on to me and headed out West to ring the bells at the Pearly Gates.

When I arrived here with all my fancy frocks and frills, the whole town turned out to meet me. This place was ripe alright. These woman-starved critters had all but fergotten what it was like to be round the opposite sex. They had lost what manners their mamas had taught em cause they had nothing to practice on. Mostly, they weren't bad men, jes in need of a little companionship. There was all kinds of sparks flyin over my favors as you could imagine. Little Belly rang high and low. There was music in the air, and it sounded like Heaven's own refrain to these poor depraved creatures. Too many men in one place is bad news. You jes gotta mix in some females to mellow the stew. It gives em something to fight about besides money and politics. Fightin over a woman ain't no better, but if'n yer gonna fight anyway, I might as well put some of that money in my pocket.

Anyway, I soon had this place looking like home with my lace curtains and velvet couches from Mama's house in Boston. Once I got the place lookin good and the bar well stocked, I opened fer business. At first it was jes me workin, but before long I had a nice full house of "languid ladies."

Many folks has passed through these Pearly Gates. The men who behaved badly got thrown out, but the women who behaved badly got rich.

After all these many years of runnin the best little whorehouse in the West, I'm sittin pretty with my little Belle Ringers. We all got our ups and downs, but mostly we're always ready fer a good time, Gents. Any way you want it.

I suck up a little of this here rot gut, and sometimes I get a little too philosophical. When I get to talking about "liberty and justice fer all," I get pretty heated up. Them are great words, but I don't see much of it happenin. Seems to me like the more liberty we're promised, the less justice we get. You can jes ferget about the part "fer all" cause that ain't how it works. Them politicians in Washington has got their heads so far up their arses they ain't never seen the light of day. What's the matter with them idiots? Do they think we're all stupid or something? Well, maybe we are. We let em lead us right into Hell.

As you can tell, I don't much like some of those government people. People say my girls are doin somethin sinful, but I think those politicians are much naughtier than any of my doves ever thought of bein. As Liberty Belle, I may be cracked but I can still ring out fer justice. It sounds a little less true, but I'll keep ringin till the day I'm liberated and the final justice is me passin through God's Pearly Gates and I'm waving to you from the other side.

You can dance at the Gate jes so long and then you gotta get past that guy who's takin names and givin out wings. Course, it could be that no amount of dancin outside is gonna get you inside. Some of us jes ain't meant fer Heaven. I figure that's up to the guy at the big desk. He's gonna check us out and check us in based on what's in our hearts, not fer what mankind decides is a sin. I sure hope my name is on that list cause I need a long rest. These girls of mine is a chore to manage. I'm ready to retire to the ranch.

A few years back, one of my favorite Gents, Rusty Cogs, fell off his last perch, and he left me his whole spread. I knowed my girls would be needin to get outta the business before too long. Beauty don't last forever. Old Rusty's ranch was my doves' retirement plan. We all got a place there to call home. Some of my girls prefer the company of animals to men. I won't say which ones cause it might spoil yer pleasure. And, Gents, yer pleasure is my business.

Chapter 12

Marge Le Barge

Marge Le Barge

I would like ya to meet my long-time friend who is here fer a visit. We like to talk over old times when she and Bill deliver a new batch of booze. This here is Marge, or Margaret Le Farge as she was known in her youth. Marge was a zestful maid with fine hopes and dreams of marryin a good-hearted man with an understandin of her need to party. As a young'un, she was raised by her preacherman uncle after her mama died of consumption. I think it was more like what she consumed.

Bein a fun-lovin wench she set out West to seek her fortune. The men out West weren't too picky about a lady's virtue. They jes didn't have time fer courtin and such. They jes wanted a good time. Marge saw that there was a place fer her out West, and she heard the cry "go West young girl, go West." So she hooked up with a wagon train headed out of St. Louis and hooker'd her way west. The Gents took a shine to her so she found plenty of wagons to hitch a ride on, but they jes didn't last long cause the wives got too uppity. They finally all got together and one mornin when Marge was pretty hung over, and they dumped her bag and baggage on the doorstep of the Pearly

Gates. This seems to be where all fallen angels end up sooner or later. She noticed that there were lots of Gents comin and goin through the Pearly Gates so this might be where she would find the man of her dreams. Meantime, it looked like a darn good party.

Over the years of workin at the Pearly Gates, Marge's youthful beauty has kinda settled to the bottom of the glass. Which is where Bill the bargeman found her one night. He had a habit of lookin through the bottom of an empty glass at the pretty ladies. He called it his "good-lookin glass." One night, after a full night of drinkin, his bloodshot eyes settled on Marge through the "good-lookin glass."

Marge has them thighs of lead and when he looked at her he saw an anchor for his love boat. Bill runs the barge that brings whiskey from the East and takes furs back. It's a lonely job, pole'n up river, and he often needed help. Bill said Marge looked like she could pole his barge all the way up river and when he needed to put ashore she'd be good fer anchorin the barge. A man needs a good woman to anchor him in life so he don't drift in the current. Marge and Bill fell in love that night, and I could see it was a match made in Heaven (or the Pearly Gates, which some men think is the same place). One of my angels was about to spread her wings and take flight.

We had a big combination retirement and weddin party fer Marge and Bill that lasted three days. It's a good idea to quit while yer still lookin good and still got some parties left in ya. What a party that was! Ole Marge slung off her corset as a symbol of her freedom and swore never to imprison her bountiful figure in that tourniquet of torture again. Bill found a good use for it though. It would make a dandy hammock fer the little barge rats he planned on sire'n. Which was okay with Marge cause she was ready to rock the cradle.

I always enjoy Bill's deliveries, but even better is my dear friend Marge Le Barge comin to party with us girls. No one parties like Marge. Bill brings out the good whiskey and we all have a rip-roarin time like only Marge can stir up. Marge still looks good through Bill's "good-lookin glass."

First loves are good, but last loves are better.

I'd like to announce our first official beauty pageant here at the Pearly Gates.

The girls are always fightin over who's the prettiest, so we're havin a contest to settle it once and fer all. We're choosin some judges so, if you'd like to try out fer the job, see Ting. She's in charge of runnin things as usual.

I'm gonna be officiating cause somebody's gotta control these high-spirited fillies. Of course, I think all of my angels is beauties, and talent abounds. Why, you can jes see fer yerself how my words don't even do em justice. It's gonna be a night to remember for sure. The girls will be hookin up their best boots and lacin up their tightest corsets fer this one.

You'll notice that Marge here is not participatin in the contest. The only runway she walks nowadays is on Bill's barge with a pole in her hand. She swore off beauty years ago. She don't miss that addiction. You see, Marge is beauty-challenged and it never came easy fer her. What she lacks in beauty she makes up fer with charm.

You see, Gents, when all else fails, charm can win out over beauty jes cause it lasts longer. When beauty slides down hill and yer back forty becomes yer lower sixty, yer charm is ripenin like a fine wine. You finally learned to keep yer mouth shut and yer legs open. Now tell me, Gents, ain't that charmin!

Marge is gonna be in charge of the party afterwards when the awards is handed out. The winner gets to be Queen fer the Night and rule over her handmaidens. Then, you Gents get to haggle over who gets a Handmaiden Heaven fer the evenin.

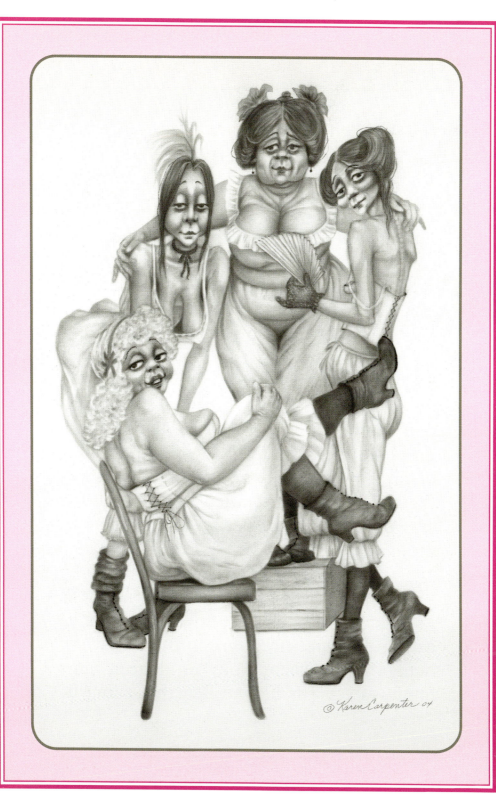

© Karen Carpenter 04

Belle's Advice

Folks is always askin me fer advice. That and my listenin and attention is about the only things round here that I give out fer free. Some folks jes love to gossip about me. Their noses is all worn down from stickin em in other people's business. They're always wonderin what I'm really all about.

The boys tell me I got a way with roundin up all them words and slappin a brand on em. Some call me an old slapper, and I guess they're referrin to my brandin. Some of my boys jes want me to listen to them talkin. They like the lovin from my ladies, but they like my special attention even more.

A hanker'n is different from a need. Ya need certain things to survive, and once ya get em ya don't need em no more, but the hanker'n jes keeps goin no matter how much ya get. It's like an itch that cain't be scratched away. The more ya get, the more ya want, and that's why my business has been around since the beginnin of time. I'm sure that a cavewoman learned quickly about the only gift God gave her to survive, and she learned to take full advantage of every hanker'n a man could come up with.

Men'll make fools outta themselves if'n ya give em half a chance. Course, it don't take a woman to make a fool outta a man. All it takes is payday and Saturday night and he'll do a good job of that himself. Men look forward to payday all week, but mostly it's exactly what they shoulda been lookin out for.

A woman learned to use her talents to get a grip on man's rampant hanker'ns. Course some of us girls is better'n others at grippin hank, but it don't take no diploma to yank hank. I educate all my girls in the old-fashioned hands-on method. Mostly, though, we jes need to show up.

A man hears what he wants to hear, and everything else is jes a waste of his time. I instruct my girls in the fine art of conversation with a man, no more than three words at a time. If a man says he wants to have a long talk, ya better be ready fer a long listen. So, I say take care of business first and then, if it jars something loose, listenin may be a way of gettin a bonus. After all, if he pays fer ten minutes, he's gonna have about eight minutes to talk, which is plenty of time fer him to say everything he knows. Eight minutes of whine'n is about all a lady can handle. Some men like to hear themselves talk more than yankin doodle dandy.

Hope, like beds, springs eternal. And jes like beds, hopes have their ups and downs, which after a while of goin up and down git pretty loosened up and worn down. Course, like beds, the bounce-backs get slower with age. Too many bounce-backs takes its toll on the old body.

Most men is jes too ornery to use a whip on, so some folks'll jes tell ya ta shoot em, but you can be hanged fer that even if the world would be better off minus a few ornery critters.

Nobody likes to do tricks fer treats, but we all do it and we use whatever talents we have to get us there. When you kin use yer talents well, you minimize yer tricks and maximize yer treats.

I think men began usin body parts fer dis-playin their feelins, cause they have so much trouble finding the right words when they get riled up. It's jes easier ta whip it, flip it, and flash it. One little gesture can say a lotta words, and a smart lady understands what's bein said.

Sometimes a pat on the head and a scratch on the behind is jes what some of these old dogs need. Cowboys kinda like gittin a full belly, and good ole boys likes jes sittin and talking on the porch in the evening sunset.

I bet you'd like to know the secret to my success. It's simple, really, and it works fer anyone. If'n ya ain't gettin what ya want outta life and yer feelin like a total failure, yer probably right. Fer instance, let's say yer sittin in yer little shack on the outskirts of town. The walls got cracks big enough fer packrats to pass through four abreast and pullin chariots. Food's so scarce yer tryin to find new ways to make beans and yer only dreamin of a little side pork or coffee. You gotta fight the spiders, fleas, and bedbugs fer the old blanket, which has so many holes in it you could use it to see daylight through. The only thing with more holes is the clothes yer wearin and the four walls holdin back the cold. You can get used to bein alone but not to bein lonely, and lonely is jes what ya got plenty of.

Yer feelin plenty sorry fer yerself fer bein such a failure. All yer fine hopes and dreams is long fergotten along with all them friends who left cause they couldn't stand yer grouchy, complainin arse. They left ya lonely and miserable to cuss at yer darned ole leaky roof alone with only the rats to listen to yer woes.

After a while, you get to where you expect to fail. Big expectations is grand fer dreamin, but when it comes down to livin a good life, maybe yer needs are more important. Sometimes, lowering yer expectations can bring you instant success. Let's say, fer example, you lower em down to below what you have. Instead of frustration, you can be happy cause you got more than you expected. Yer cup runneth over. Now, yer a man of means and can offer to take in that "old, over-the-hill squaw woman" that people in town been kickin around fer months.

Jes think about livin in a tent on the side of a hill with the temperature of below zero and nothin to eat but the soup of boiled shoe leather worn by an old dead miner ten years ago. With thinkin like this, yer shack begins to look like home, sweet home.

Now yer a success story, and you begin feelin like a winner with enough confidence to attract that squaw woman who wanders through town looking for who-knows-what. Turns out, she jes loves cleanin and polishin and listenin and can find more ways of cookin up beans than you ever dreamed of. She even adds some fresh venison fer a real feast.

Now yer sittin back in yer chair in that same shack with a grateful squaw woman who really knows how to listen and loves to light yer pipe. Things is lookin mighty fine. Same story, different ending. At last you have what you need to be happy and some-one to share it with, and all ya had to do was change yer expectations and love what life gives you a little more.

I always tell my ladies who jes cain't seem to find a good man that

Number One: All men are created equal. They jes seem to be idiots but, as in all things, some are worse idiots than others; and

Number Two: If'n ya cain't find what ya want, want what ya find.

Trouble here is that some girls had so many idiots to choose from they got con-fused about what they were lookin fer and don't know what to expect. They don't know what's "for better or worse" than what they got. They get lost in the sediment at the bottom of the jug.

When I find girls like this, I bring um here to the Pearly Gates and show em how they're all angels who deserve to have their wings. They jes need to find what's good in their lives. We all see what's "wrong" cause it makes us uncomfortable. Maybe that's a stronger feelin than comfort. When those ole biddies in town get to thinkin we ladies are bad fer givin a little pleasure to love-starved men, we get to believin em. We may make lovin easy fer Gents, but that ain't necessarily bad. Sometimes the only love available is what you can hire, and at least it's better than no love. No love makes folks hard and cold.

Me and my kind is jes like a lot of people. We're all whores for something: sex, money, alcohol, power, social position. None of us is "better or worse" than anyone else. We jes each arrive on different roads, and some of us come to the doorsteps of the Pearly Gates as Deservin Angels.

There is something to be said fer experience. When you got as much as I got doin anything, yer gonna be great at what you do. Now don't it make sense to pay fer the best when you got a hanker'n. Otherwise, you'll never be satisfied. I'm built to satisfy, honey!

Many have passed through Belle's Pearly Gates, and there's a reason why them gates swing both ways. So behave yerself or Belle's gonna shows you the outside of them gates and there won't be any chimes ringin in yer ears.

Liberty Belle

Myrt

Gert

Muddy Mary

Sophie

Poleaalotus

Mae Bea Laid

Fifi

Violet

Effie

Goldie

Marge Le Barge

Belle's Order Form

As most of you Gents know, I'm a serious business-woman. I ain't no tool shed hoe that gits hung up on a hook. Like most ladies, I like ta be remembered, so we got some nice pictures here of me and some of my girls. I hope they bring ya a smile to lift up yer cheeks. Everbody needs a cheek lifter once in a while or they git too serious, right boys?

You can have yer very own set of pictures of us ladies in all our glory. And we'll be smilin down at ya from the Pearly Gates. And you can smile right back at us.

My lips have lifted many cheeks and should be famous by now. There's been many Gents ta carry home a lip smack on their collars fer a souvenir. It sure sets tongues ta waggin.

Now, y'all can take home a T-shirt with a remembrance of yer favorite lady on the back, and one of my special lip smacks on the front. Git one fer yer lady to wear, and when she turns her back on ya, ya kin see yer favorite dove looking back at ya. That'll lift up yer cheeks with a smile and that, in turn, will warm up the chilly mood of yer own lady. "It's a good thing ta do," as my mama would way.

To help our retirement fund, please order from one of Belle's old time helpers. The order form is on the next page. It'll put a smile on yer face and some bounce-back in your step.

Order Form for

Naughty Ladies of the Pearly Gates

Book, Prints, and T-shirts

Item	Lady Code	Color Code	Size	Qty	Price	Total
Naughty Ladies of the Pearly Gates					$15.95 ea	
T-shirt (women)					$19.95 ea	
T-shirt (men)					$19.95 ea	
Prints 9 ˇ 12 (set of 12)					$24.95	
Utah residents add 6.6% sales tax						
Shipping and handling						
					Total	$

T-shirts (100% cotton) are available in a choice of 3 colors: oatmeal (code: **O**), pink (**P**), and sage (**S**).
Adult sizes: M, L, XL, and XXL.
Available Ladies: Young Liberty Belle (code: **B**), Sophie (**S**), Pokesalotus (**P**), Violet (**V**), Mae Bea (**M**), and Fifi (**F**).

A complete set of 12 prints (one of each lady) printed in duotone on 9 ˇ 12 card stock suitable for framing.

Shipping and Handling Add: $4.00 for orders $25.00 or less.
$7.00 for orders $25 to $50.
$10.00 for orders $50 to $100.
$15.00 for orders $100 or more.

Make checks or money orders payable to:

Tobacco River Ranch
1818 West 2300 South,
West Valley City, UT 84119

Check will be held for clearance prior to shipping. Allow 14 days for delivery.
For wholesale or rush orders, please call 1-801-886-8824

Name: _____

Address: _____ Phone: _____

City: _____ State: _____ Zip: _____

Shipping address (if different from above): _____

_____

Order Form for

Naughty Ladies of the Pearly Gates

Book, Prints, and T-shirts

Item	Lady Code	Color Code	Size	Qty	Price	Total
Naughty Ladies of the Pearly Gates					$15.95 ea	
T-shirt (women)					$19.95 ea	
T-shirt (men)					$19.95 ea	
Prints 9 ˇ 12 (set of 12)					$24.95	
Utah residents add 6.6% sales tax						
Shipping and handling						
					Total	$

T-shirts (100% cotton) are available in a choice of 3 colors: oatmeal (code: **O**), pink (**P**), and sage (**S**).
Adult sizes: M, L, XL, and XXL.
Available Ladies: Young Liberty Belle (code: **B**), Sophie (**S**), Pokesalotus (**P**), Violet (**V**), Mae Bea (**M**), and Fifi (**F**).

A complete set of 12 prints (one of each lady) printed in duotone on 9 ˇ 12 card stock suitable for framing.

Shipping and Handling Add: $4.00 for orders $25.00 or less.
$7.00 for orders $25 to $50.
$10.00 for orders $50 to $100.
$15.00 for orders $100 or more.

Make checks or money orders payable to:

Tobacco River Ranch
1818 West 2300 South,
West Valley City, UT 84119

Check will be held for clearance prior to shipping. Allow 14 days for delivery.
For wholesale or rush orders, please call 1-801-886-8824

Name: _____

Address: _____ Phone: _____

City: _____ State: _____ Zip: _____

Shipping address (if different from above): _____

_____

Order Form for

Naughty Ladies of the Pearly Gates

Book, Prints, and T-shirts

Item	Lady Code	Color Code	Size	Qty	Price	Total
Naughty Ladies of the Pearly Gates					$15.95 ea	
T-shirt (women)					$19.95 ea	
T-shirt (men)					$19.95 ea	
Prints 9 ˜ 12 (set of 12)					$24.95	
Utah residents add 6.6% sales tax						
Shipping and handling						
					Total	$

T-shirts (100% cotton) are available in a choice of 3 colors: oatmeal (code: **O**), pink (**P**), and sage (**S**).
Adult sizes: M, L, XL, and XXL.
Available Ladies: Young Liberty Belle (code: **B**), Sophie (**S**), Pokesalotus (**P**), Violet (**V**), Mae Bea (**M**), and Fifi (**F**).

A complete set of 12 prints (one of each lady) printed in duotone on 9 ˜ 12 card stock suitable for framing.

Shipping and Handling Add: $4.00 for orders $25.00 or less.
$7.00 for orders $25 to $50.
$10.00 for orders $50 to $100.
$15.00 for orders $100 or more.

Make checks or money orders payable to:

Tobacco River Ranch
1818 West 2300 South,
West Valley City, UT 84119

Check will be held for clearance prior to shipping. Allow 14 days for delivery.
For wholesale or rush orders, please call 1-801-886-8824

Name: _____

Address: _____ Phone: _____

City: _____ State: _____ Zip: _____

Shipping address (if different from above): _____

_____

Order Form for

Naughty Ladies of the Pearly Gates

Book, Prints, and T-shirts

Item	Lady Code	Color Code	Size	Qty	Price	Total
Naughty Ladies of the Pearly Gates					$15.95 ea	
T-shirt (women)					$19.95 ea	
T-shirt (men)					$19.95 ea	
Prints 9 ˘ 12 (set of 12)					$24.95	
Utah residents add 6.6% sales tax						
Shipping and handling						
					Total	$

T-shirts (100% cotton) are available in a choice of 3 colors: oatmeal (code: **O**), pink (**P**), and sage (**S**).
Adult sizes: M, L, XL, and XXL.
Available Ladies: Young Liberty Belle (code: **B**), Sophie (**S**), Pokesalotus (**P**), Violet (**V**), Mae Bea (**M**), and Fifi (**F**).

A complete set of 12 prints (one of each lady) printed in duotone on 9 ˘ 12 card stock suitable for framing.

Shipping and Handling Add: $4.00 for orders $25.00 or less.
$7.00 for orders $25 to $50.
$10.00 for orders $50 to $100.
$15.00 for orders $100 or more.

Make checks or money orders payable to:

Tobacco River Ranch
1818 West 2300 South,
West Valley City, UT 84119

Check will be held for clearance prior to shipping. Allow 14 days for delivery.
For wholesale or rush orders, please call 1-801-886-8824

Name: _____ _____

Address: _____ Phone: _____

City: _____ State: _____ Zip: _____

Shipping address (if different from above): _____

_____

Order Form for

Naughty Ladies of the Pearly Gates

Book, Prints, and T-shirts

Item	Lady Code	Color Code	Size	Qty	Price	Total
Naughty Ladies of the Pearly Gates					$15.95 ea	
T-shirt (women)					$19.95 ea	
T-shirt (men)					$19.95 ea	
Prints 9 ˜ 12 (set of 12)					$24.95	
Utah residents add 6.6% sales tax						
Shipping and handling						
					Total	$

T-shirts (100% cotton) are available in a choice of 3 colors: oatmeal (code: **O**), pink (**P**), and sage (**S**).
Adult sizes: M, L, XL, and XXL.
Available Ladies: Young Liberty Belle (code: **B**), Sophie (**S**), Pokesalotus (**P**), Violet (**V**), Mae Bea (**M**), and Fifi (**F**).

A complete set of 12 prints (one of each lady) printed in duotone on 9 ˜ 12 card stock suitable for framing.

Shipping and Handling Add: $4.00 for orders $25.00 or less.
$7.00 for orders $25 to $50.
$10.00 for orders $50 to $100.
$15.00 for orders $100 or more.

Make checks or money orders payable to:

Tobacco River Ranch
1818 West 2300 South,
West Valley City, UT 84119

Check will be held for clearance prior to shipping. Allow 14 days for delivery.

For wholesale or rush orders, please call 1-801-886-8824

Name: _____

Address: _____ Phone: _____

City: _____ State: _____ Zip: _____

Shipping address (if different from above): _____

_____